A Pen Pal for Max

A Pen Pal for Max

Gloria Rand

ILLUSTRATED BY Ted Rand

Henry Holt and Company

New York

Henry Holt and Company, LLC
Publishers since 1866
115 West 18th Street
New York, New York 10011
www.henryholt.com

Library of Congress Cataloging-in-Publication Data
Rand, Gloria.
A pen pal for Max / Gloria Rand; illustrated by Ted Rand.—1st ed.
p.   cm.
Summary: The young son of a Chilean farmer writes a note asking for a "faraway friend,"
and places it in a box of grapes bound for the United States.
ISBN-13: 978-0-8050-7586-1
ISBN-10: 0-8050-7586-0
[1. Pen pals—Fiction. 2. Chile—Fiction.] I. Rand, Ted, ill. II. Title.
PZ7.R1553Pe 2005   [E]—dc22   2004024283

First Edition—2005 / Designed by Amy Manzo Toth
Printed in the United States of America on acid-free paper. ∞

1 3 5 7 9 10 8 6 4 2

To our dear friends
Patricia and Juan Oehninger
of El Monte, Chile

Maximiliano lived in a small house on a huge fruit farm in Chile, South America. The farm belonged to Don Manuel. Max's father worked in the farm's vineyard. That's where grapes were grown to be shipped to markets all over the world.

Max liked living on Don Manuel's farm. He had his own pony there and many friends nearby.

One day Max rode his pony over to the farm's packing house to watch as large wooden bins, each filled with newly harvested grapes, were brought in from the vineyards. He stayed to see the grapes separated into small bunches, wrapped in paper, and put into boxes. These boxes were quickly stacked in waiting trucks for the short ride to a nearby seaport, where they would be loaded onto refrigerated freighters and shipped to many different countries.

"Want to go along for the ride?" the packing house manager jokingly asked Max. "These grapes are about to leave for the United States. Do you have any friends there?"

Max had none. And that's when he got the idea that it would be fun to have a friend in a faraway place. Quickly he turned his pony around and headed home. As soon as he got there he secretly wrote this note:

In English it read: "Hello, my name is Maximiliano Farias. I would like to be your friend. Please write to me." He signed his name and gave his address.

Max tucked the note into his shirt pocket and rode back to the packing house, where grapes were still being brought in and prepared for shipping. When no one was looking, Max slipped the note into a box of grapes.

"Maybe someone will find this," Max said to himself. "Maybe that person will write an answer to me and we can become friends."

Max told no one about the note, not even his little sister, but he often asked his mother, "Was there any mail for me today?"

"Are you expecting a letter?" his mother always asked.

"No, not really."

Weeks and weeks went by. Just when Max had about given up thinking that anyone would ever answer, a letter addressed to Maximiliano arrived at the house.

"Is this why you've been asking about the mail?" Max's mother looked puzzled as she handed him the envelope. "This is from someone in the United States. I can tell by the stamp. What in the world have you been up to, Max?"

As he ripped open the envelope, Max told his mother about the note he'd put into a box of grapes. Then in a disappointed voice he said, "Oh, no. Look at this. I've gotten a letter I can't read."

Max's mother recognized that the letter was written in English, even though she could not read it herself.

"Don Manuel speaks and writes the English language. Maybe if you ask nicely, he'll translate this letter for you."

Max hurried down the dusty road to Don Manuel's house. The housekeeper answered his knock on the mansion's impressive front door.

"Come along," she said as she led Max into a grand room where Don Manuel was enjoying a late-afternoon cup of tea.

"Hello, Max. What brings you here?" Don Manuel asked.

Max explained about his secret note.

"Well, what an interesting thing to do." Don Manuel smiled. "Hand me the letter and I'll read it to you."

The letter was from a girl named Maggie. She explained that her father was the produce manager at a large grocery store in a big city in the United States. He'd found Max's note as he was opening up boxes of Chilean grapes.

"My father brought your note home and told me to take it to school. He was sure my teacher, Ms. Moore, who is also the school's Spanish teacher, could read it for me. Ms. Moore did, and she thinks you might be about my age. I'm ten years old," Maggie explained. "Are you ten years old, too? Write back."

That evening Max wrote to Maggie. Then Maggie wrote back to Max. They became regular pen pals. They wrote to each other often.

They wrote about school, soccer games, and their hobbies. They wrote about what they'd like to be when they grew up. They wrote about the weather where they lived and how when it was summer in South America, it was winter in North America. They even wrote about how bothersome little brothers and sisters could be.

Don Manuel was always glad to translate for Max, and that's what he was doing one day when there was a loud rumbling sound and his big house began to shake. Furniture tumbled, vases and lamps crashed to the floor, tiles fell off the roof, and a cloud of dust rose up around everything. It was a terrible earthquake.

"Come on!" Don Manuel cried out as he grabbed Max's hand. Together they ran out into the garden, dodging falling parts of the old farm mansion.

"Here, hang on to me," Don Manuel yelled over the din of the quake, trying to stay on his feet out in the middle of a large lawn that was heaving up and down. "You'll be fine, just hang on. This shaking is sure to stop soon."

In the distance Max could see his pony running down the dirt road toward home. He wanted to run home, too, but Don Manuel said that wasn't a good idea. Debris was still crashing down everywhere.

"Stay right here until the earth quiets down," he told Max. "It won't be long."

As soon as the ground seemed to be moving less, Don Manuel said, "It's okay to go on home now. Your mother is probably worried sick. Hurry! Just don't get near any of the farm buildings in case more tiles fall from the roofs!"

Max reached his house in record time, just as his father was returning from the vineyards. His mother and sister, who had been at home during the whole horrible earthquake, hugged them both. They were all very happy to be together but still badly frightened by the force of the rumbling earth.

The next day Max learned that his school was closed because it had so many broken windows and large cracks in the walls. It would take weeks for the needed repairs to be made. Since the earth was still trembling and moving now and then, Max was glad to be home.

After a while the quake became only a scary memory, and Max went back to school.

"There's a nice surprise waiting for you here, Max," the school principal said as he pointed to a pile of boxes outside Max's classroom door. "These are all addressed to you and your classmates."

With the principal, the teacher, and the kids in his class helping, Max opened up box after box. They were filled with books, games, paper, pens, and even new clothes. In one box there was a picture of his friend Maggie and her classmates, along with a short letter.

Hi! Max—

And hi to all the kids in your class at school. We hope none of you got hurt in the earthquake. When you have time to write us, we'd really like to know how you are and what it was like. In case your stuff got wrecked, we're sending you some new stuff.

From your faraway friends,

Maggie

Haley Laura Jason Olivia Holly Matthew

Marc

Alexa

Tyler

Chloe

Emma

Brittany Jordan Esmeralda Maggie Kendra Kelly H.
Kolton Austin Dakota Shawn

Aaron Tony Addison

Max was really pleased. The note he'd put into a box
of grapes had found a faraway friend, not only for himself
but for his whole class, too.